DEV-OCEAN

Lucaz Abrams

First Printing: 2016
Publisher:
M F J Wicks
P.O. Box 1573, Thuringowa Central,
Qld, Australia 4817
Cover Art by M F J Wicks
www.abrams-dev-ocean.com.au

phone: +61 07 47736536
legal name: M. F. J. Wicks

SC ISBN 978-0-9944403-1-0
EB ISBN 978-0-9944403-2-7

Lulu Publishing Services rev. date: 7/1/2016

Since the beginning of civilisation, humanity has romanced about the Whales, Dolphins and even Sharks as mysterious creatures of the sea. They feature in artwork, poetry, mythology and legends of many nations for their unique traits and the intrigue of their secret lives beneath the waves. Until recently, we could only observe them on the surface but nowadays, modern technology lets us build a picture of their habits below the waves so we can virtually be on-board when a whale hunts for quarry in the deepest abyss or be part of the dynamic coral reef action.

CONTENTS

SOULITUDE

Mid-Ocean, Mid-Morning, Fog-Bound.

Damn, it's the seaman's curse; still air and a lifeless helm. I'm floating in a gossamer mist; is it the sea or sky?

I can only hear and sense the gentle lap and wash of that steely sea. No division of sea and sky; my world is engulfed by that opaque haze, leaving no definition to fix my position by. Do I imagine that steely slinky sea is it looking back at me? Maybe a mesmerising glare, a frown, I fear!

"Come join me! Come join me!" A slippery behemoth of the hidden sea seems to taunt me, "Your soporific soul will be free!"

"Why me? A single-handed sailor: the lonely skipper of a wave cutter in a solitary sea with only that thickening white infinity to beat." My inner-voice rebels.

Is it just a dare or should I care? I feel invited by a persistent gaze from an ancient traveller that plies this aquamarine vacancy. Darn those distant courting tunes and resonant clicks: why should they bother me? It's an open seaway!

So absorbed in thought am I, musing about that slippery behemoth of the sea and sky, it unites our essential minds as one, to be free, to frolic unhindered in a sine-wave sea. Together we roam that liquid space, serenaded by sonic refrains from near and far, of groaning romantic-blues, haunting ballad squeals and cultured yelps. A mystic opera of ancient Cetacean overtures performed by vocalists unknown, flowing with the current shifts in a submerged studio. I'm becoming attuned to that giant whose soul has adopted me.

I feel its strength, stamina and polar sourced energy as it surges north instinctively. Then I hear its echoing coda clicks, the staccato song that announces its presence to a friendly nursery pod. With the power of joy it breaches from the sea and slaps its mighty flukes to signal a return from inbred solitude. I witness a natural ballet of social harmony, as it performs a courting waltz with selected company. No boredom here, with rolling, diving, head lunging, slapping of flippers and flukes or just basking on an undulating seascape. I'm with a genial socialite, grand champion of a seaworthy sorority.

Then I sense a subtle change, a more serious mood that rejects the zealous pleasures of surface life when it heads for a distant horizon with extra vigour. It charges through the ocean swells and is soon beyond the continental shelf, then continues underwater as if acquainted with every submerged path in this three-dimensional blue; oh my, is it preparing for a deep-water dive?

From beneath that enveloping, turbid sea it bursts, to breathe and breathe again sixfold, of our atmosphere's life-giving air; lungs full it descends slowly, buoyant in the viscous hue - I contemplate its view of schooling fish and predators too.

"I feel welcome but should I be here?" I object, knowing my thoughts and concerns are foreign to its placid, carefree, spontaneity. "The Great White Shark is less an enemy than me, why must I continue this euphotic odyssey?"

Uh-hol! We're diving, no time to plead; it's heading for forbidden territory. Aa-agh! It's taking me into those murky depths of immediate privacy and unlocking the mystery of a double life, flirting with danger in an undersea chasm. Its aerobic flukes are thrusting, driving us deeper…, dee-eeper, ever dee-ee-eeper, away from the rituals of nektonic activity, past the last vestige of light and into a briny hell. It plummets further still and greets the lung crushing abyssal depths, 1500 fathoms at least; a hold-breath diver unhindered by the compressing darkness, where the twilight ends and shadows cease to exist. Down here, we are unseen, camouflaged by the perpetual night. Its vital heart pulse reduced, unneeded metabolism suppressed and minimum effort expended for directional control. "It's at home here, while I'm searching the depths of my soul," I ponder.

Now we're on a level trajectory, an abyssal plain for sure. It pauses and surveys that imposing gloom for an instant snack or possibly an ocean floor feast. With no time to waste, its jaw engages the sandy-muddy ooze and ploughs a trench, disturbing hidden octopods, starfish and crabs; tasty appetisers quickly consumed as a prelude to the main course pursuit. With a lunge of its powerful tail we launch into that unforgiving trench once more and cruise stealthily, on a secret mission to catch its opponent by surprise. I'm humbled by its unwavering strength of purpose, consoled by the warmth of its athletic flesh and bone that shields me from the bitter cold and ever-present danger from all around but it sure ain't the security of steel.

"I didn't care for these creatures that roam this watery space; a likely reason for this confounded dare," my inner thoughts declare. Is that why I'm observing a carbon black world through a cetacean's elliptical eye and sensing the squeezing of body sleek as it searches for Giant Squid; its venison of the very deep? Then I hear it sounding that limitless abyss with overpowering echolocation clicks, sweep after sweep and feel the inner-tension of hunting for hidden prey. No defined shapes down here, just photophore outlines, luminescent plates, ghostly incarnates that are for a fleeting moment seen. How can anything exist in an icy cold underworld?

The shadow of an echo sent returns, revealing a helpless prey stunned and paralysed by concentrated blasts of clicks; it's unable to retreat. There's the dampened noise of a desperate skirmish; the flailing, writhing tentacles of a Giant Squid embrace a fearless crusader of the deep-sea abyss. I wince at the ferocity of the fight and a sickening notion crosses my mind; "Could this be the end; did it have to involve me?"

The behemoth's jaws take hold as those suction-grip tentacles probe, beat, push or punish like a whip as a kingly denizen defends, then with a muffled groan it quickly submits to a superior foe; defeated in that insulating sea. It's nice to feel protected inside that master class diving suit that bears the scars of many deep-sea conflicts. "Who would challenge its right to enjoy that meal?" Is my admiring thought as it feeds unseen by other mortal souls where only the strongest of all will stay alive?

Hunger satisfied, oxygen balance in the red, it thrusts upwards to escape the restricting darkness. With only gravity to beat and making haste through the mid-depth gloom, it looks for the radiant blue: the magnetism of a lighted view.

"Oh! Such overwhelming joy," I celebrate. Real life is visible as we emerge from that murky hue and leave behind the featureless, languid depths of a primal sea. Now looking for some revitalising air, it ignores stealthy and complacent Sharks, glides through glinting silver Tuna shoals, past sprinting Manta Rays and fast-forwards into the vibrant cosmopolitan life of the sun-lit zone.

Eco-cultured ballads and minstrel blues herald our joyful return but as I listen to those syntonic notes there's a foreign distant call, a hollow mournful echo, so faint it can just be heard in that brightening sea. The behemoth's mood changes as we zero-in on the radiance above, for a moment slowing then it keeps going; a playful pod is nearby and their homely sonar clicks beckon its return.

Suddenly, we're in friendly blue-green territory and within range of those mellow background songs but that foreign call persists and it's a little louder too. Those frigid depths are just a memory, as this oceanic raider and I feel the welcoming warmth of the surface waters where the daylight glow promises a more real world. My spirit lifts as we cruise amongst Manta Rays and Dolphins but there's that foreign call again and it's a bit closer too; what can it possibly be? A more familiar note than before, bringing forth a little fear. With no time to look or worry, we glide up to the mirrored under-surface of a waveless sea and I wonder;

will that enclosing mist still hinder us? My living diving suit reduces the angle of ascent and pace to break the surface gently, then gives a lung-clearing spout and inhales a fresh supply of invigorating atmosphere. Boy, we surely enjoy that first breath and a few more too.

"Oh No! Drat it! We've emerged in that same ghostly expanse," I grumble because there's still no division between the sea and sky.

"That foreign distant echo should be much clearer no… What the heck… Where am… *OH HELL! STREWTH, I must have drifted into a dreamy sleep. BLOOM'N FO-OG! THE WHEE-EL!*" Suddenly awake and panic stricken I spring to the helm.

'BLEEE-EEE-UUU-UUR' That fearful echo is bearing down on me. It's solemn song reflects from all around, as if a mythical triton trumpets with his conch shell to becalm the salty sea in this mystical amphitheatre. **'BLEEE-EEE-UUU-UUR'** *"OH MY GOSH, another warning pulse and louder now."* Without a skerrick of wind to push me clear that infernal call instils a dread of hidden danger I can only hear! Darn that deep abyssal dream, now it's a menacing nightmare for real.

"Which bleeding way should I steer?" is my frustrated cry as I impatiently wait for that iron titan's fog-probing bellow to shatter the silence again. It sounds lonesome and forlorn behind an opaline sky, but from which direction is so unclear, this sleepy sea has its own way of haunting me. "Hah-hah, that's it; I'll point my arm towards the centre of that sudden mournful sound to find a heading for a danger unseen."

'BLEEE-EEE-UUU-UUR' Drat, that resounding song is much louder and nearly on top of me. *"For heaven's sake man use engine power to go about; at least you'll have a fighting chance and it'll reduce the closing speed!"* my thoughts scream under my breath while looking for threatening signs of an iron shadow. "It may be about ther...re, to port, a little forward of abeam but heading this way." No silence now, my ears lock onto the rhythmical 'thru-ump shi-ish, thru-ump shi-ish, thru-ump shi-ish' of propellers as the vessel approaches cautiously.

It's not the usual me that hastily fumbles for a rarely used ignition key, grabs the ship's wheel and airs a little anxiety, *"START, MOTOR, START, PLE-EA-SE, START!"* It churns and pops for a moment, then judders as it fires. **"YAHOO!"** Few would be happier to hear that muffled roar as a two pot diesel thrusts us forward; full throttle it is.

'BLEEE-EEE-UUU-UUR' "Yikes! Is this my last hurrah or not?" 'BLEE-U-UR.......BLEE-U-UR' "Short, Short; it knows I'm here and passing to port, no doubt spied by its electronic eye. Heck, that warning confirms my greatest dread, we're on a collision course," I fearfully think while spinning the wheel to starboard with the hope of reaching safety. **"HELL'S BELLS!** There it is, a towering iron freighter charging from the mist and quickly bearing down on me." To me its protruding bulbous bow is as threatening as a Roman galley's ram that sliced through the sea to maim the enemy. *"PICK UP YAH KEEL YAH OLD WAVE*

CUTTER AND ONLY LET IT SEE YAH WAKE," I yell while pressing the throttle home hard to coax every propeller driven knot from my trusty sloop as the precious seconds disappear in double quick time.

'**BLEE-U-UR……..BLEE-UU-UR'** "Short, Short again; it's steering to port a bit more, although the heading looks little different to me." Indeed, those towering traders of the world's seaways need a mile or two to turn or stop and I've inadvertently strayed into this one's path. An old salt like me would be unwise to bluff a cargo-carrying heavyweight and ignore a basic rule of the high seas. **"LUMMY!** I'm suddenly reliving the drama of an earlier close shave when silly me was inattentive, while making good speed with the benefit of a following breeze. The danger of that misadventure is still freshly imprinted on my mind."

"Oh, how I lament the recent past! A moment of anguish and despair was answered by a crusty sailor's heart-felt and spoken prayer. How else could I swallow my pride for cussing a slippery behemoth that chanced upon my path? That venting of expression brash and animated anger expounded into the air with emotion black and temper red. An urgent tack, sloop a'heel, sails a'flap, a wildly swinging boom, acutely tilting mast, the creaks of straining timber'n'steel, an almost visible keel - a certain collision was avoided. A surprise attack it appeared to be or was it the ultimate test of my seafaring ability in this blue/ green territory? Now I feel guilty of a verbal offence and my

weathered complexion's extra ruddy, knowing the sea could've been really bloody."

The scything hiss of a bow ploughing through the sea jolts me back to reality; that emerging iron shadow is about to hide the white blankness of the sky. "Now I'm reading those plimsoll marks, 111, 1V and V below a prominent line around its ocean wetted girth; that means it's only lightly loaded." At least my sloop is gaining speed as its motor strains to overcome the displacement drag with no wind assist. "Darn this idle air!" I scream.

"Will penance be lifted," I query as that bow wave sculptured from the flattest of seas lifts my trusty sloop. It pitches and rolls at close quarters, an arm span from that floating wall of steel so this anxious skipper is urgently swinging the wheel. The mast sways and the boom swings with each breaking wave until the ever louder 'throo-shi-issh, throo-shi-ishh' of the propellers tells me the danger is almost past.

Then my sloop slips into that iron titan's foamy wash stern first so this able seaman must fight for rudder control of a pitching, yawing hull. Almost instantly it's a dead flat sea again so turning towards that ocean trader, I joyfully utter as one mariner to another; "I salute you for giving way so I'll live another day," as it disappears into that opaque shroud. The echo of its sombre song is less haunting than before and seems to be celebrating our near miss.

"Phew, that could've been the end of me or was that close call a good omen instead," this overwrought yachty thinks and wipes a profusely sweating brow. "At least I'm sailing this steely slinky sea with no spectre of fear hanging over me." Then with a more humble mind I ponder; had I forgotten the true spirit of nautical lore and incurred the displeasure of an ancient deity, the immortal guardian of the seas, by heaping scorn upon his most noble whale. Did he preside over my watery trial; quelling the prevailing winds so a closed session could be convened in a misty court of the high seas? That all-powerful god of the sea looked upon my spontaneous misdeed as judge and jury; a plea of human insecurity and a later change of heart was answered with a reprimand to test my seafaring ability and sincerity. Detained in a seaworthy brig with my destiny in exalted hands, I was encouraged to atone for that vocal obscenity with a trial of aquatic hardship and an odyssey of self-discovery. My soul was spirited into that hellish abyss to let me see the courage and endeavour of a behemoth that hunts for prey in the unforgiving depths. Now blessed with newfound integrity and in retrospect I must decree, that needless profanity had echoed through the mist and offended the bravest creature of them all.

"Wow-ee, my inner self is free; I've earned a reprieve for redressing that needless negativity! It seems good fortune has smiled on me, I only wish this persistent mist would drift away."

A little wiser than before I slowly continue the voyage under motor power; keeping alert for threats that could appear from anywhere. Then, as if by magic a strong breeze lifts that ghostly fog, unmasking the real world that abounds a washboard sea and to my surprise, I've regained some living company. Shocked,

I exclaim, "I'll be a son of a gun, that slippery behemoth is escorting my sloop once more."

Pleased to be released from solitary and keen to be in step with nature this time, I eagerly reset the jib to harness a freshening breeze so we're travelling together peacefully. Now a bond of respect unites this altruistic sperm whale and me so with a cheerful heart I avow, "We share the enduring spirit of sea dogs that choose to be free."

We cruise that vast ocean space all day until the golden sunset gives way to an ever-deepening shade of grey. Then my noble companion suddenly quickens the tempo of its sinusoidal glide, dives slightly deeper and breaches with a playful splash. Is it signalling a friendly pod nearby or a polite goodbye? I happily acknowledge it as both and quickly yell a farewell, "Bon Voyage my friend, one day we'll meet'n'greet on a distant horizon," as it disappears under the waves to go a separate way.

Alone at last, I sail the open seaway under a resplendent moon that highlights the division of sea and sky. My trusty sloop makes good headway before an untamed breeze that fills the sails and powers the bow through the ocean swells. Happy now, I scan the heavenly sights for celestial signposts amongst that myriad of stars and clearly visible to my eyes, is a constellation to fix my position by.

I must joyfully say, "This is a celebration of freedom for me!"

Cetacean: Whales - Whalebone species (Rorqual and Right whales are plankton filter feeders) & Toothed species (Dolphins and Sperm whales eat fish and squid).

Euphotic (Epipelagic) Zone: The sunlit zone of the ocean to 200mt depth.

Nektonic activity: The population of sea animals such as fish, molluscs and plankton that swim or move about in the ocean independent of the currents.

Abyssal (Abyssopelagic) Zone: The midnight zone of the ocean 2000 - 4000mt where no sunlight penetrates.

MOMENTUM

"Ah-koo-koo-ah, ah-koo-koo-ah, ah-koo-koo-ah"

My sleepy eyes peep out from beneath a surf print doona and peer out the window, and that brings a curt response. "A-agh, nature's alarm clock strikes again!"

A Kookaburra has swooped on a small lizard and is celebrating the catch. Its claw securely clamps the reptile's broken body onto a still swaying branch that's just outside the half-open window at the foot of my bed.

"Ah-koo-koo-ah, Ah-koo-koo-ah"

"Here's some tough love for disturbing me," I snarl and forcefully hurl my pillow towards that source of aggravation. It hits the glass pane with a soft rattling thud instead.

The startled bird beaks the lizard and with an urgent flutter, it's gone.

"Damn! Damn! Damn! Now I'm wide awake. I hope that's not an omen for today?" I remonstrate under my breath.

The sun's glow is blitzing the horizon and its light rays are bursting through the floor to ceiling windows as a sharp edged pool of light. It creeps towards my bed and demands some attention and interest in nature's glory. So, with some reluctance I slip my legs out, sit on the bed and observe the mountaintop hijinks at this early hour.

"Let's see; Brahminy Kites hover on the breeze patiently then free-fall for a sunrise breakfast; Wonderful! Flower raiding Lorikeets flit from tree to tree and screech their optimism for this brand new day; Marvellous! Playful Rock Wallabies hop up and down the cliff face crags; carefree fun in the early hours; Great!"

"As usual, our quaint little village hasn't stirred but the harbour is busy and that o-oh so beautiful sea is where I'd love to be. Oh my, what a magical scene; the local trawlers could be shiny-shelled molluscs en route to an emerging golden bloom. Their slow-sliding silhouettes leave shiny slick trails that eventually wash into a glossy bronze-grey swell and disappear into a glowing pool of infinity. Eureka! I'm back to the good life; freedom's in sync with me again."

Unfortunately, the live entertainment is soon over and I realise there's time to kill. Getting a local newspaper or magazine would be nice but the newsagent is at the bottom of the hill and out of reach for now. I'm stranded till late afternoon; the family's gone shopping in Aspen, the nearest town with a supermarket and hardware. They left in the car while I slept off a late homecoming.

"What a bummer, my mountain bike is out of whack, courtesy of wrecker Ronnie, my younger brother." I'd normally be into my trail-blazing zone; pounding knobblies downhill and dodging rocks'n'trees on the tortuous track to the village store and back up again but alas the chain and sprocket are kaput.

"A dilemma for a free think'n guy, aye," I ponder while slapping my fave tee'n'boardies on. Then, after smashing a cereal/coffee breakfast, I hit the bbq-deck's daybed to consider the day's options.

"No sense assembling the windsurfer; a glassy sea is no fun at all. What can save me from a dreary day?" I moan while trying to conjure up a more challenging pursuit.

After graduating and benefiting from two weeks of wind surfing, I'm open to any stimulus a semi-wilderness backyard/ seaside retreat can provide but it's my first day at home so anything sporty will suffice.

"Of course; Mum and Dad said there's something special in the study!" I suddenly remember; catapulting to my feet, I beeline for it. It's supposed to be a hyper-drive computer setup and the latest extreme reality simulator. Uh-ha, there's a note with it too, *'Bret, since your more 'Tech' than 'Mech', I've assembled and setup the main unit; just plug the controller into the power, press the orange button and follow the user guide. Please arrange the rest of the gear to your liking and have fun, son.'* It should be a flame'n hoot, a budding sportsman's dream. The packaging blurb says it's THE VIRTL-XPLORR REEF DIVE simulator from Explorr Studios. Their design team worked with John & Dianne Trinder's enhanced 4D analysis of the world's major reefs to create true-life virtual reality imagery with dynamic touch/feel recognition and proximity detection for seven games with three levels of difficulty. Wow! It'll be a blast."

Without delay the modular desk is assembled, its three drawers are fitted and the virtl-xplorr controller, big-screen monitor and computer tower, laser colour printer, and all the connecting paraphernalia take pride of place on its wood-grain laminate top. Then I hurriedly place the scanner and other extras into the big bottom drawer but to my annoyance, its overfull and won't close completely.

"Damn it, I don't need to be ultra-tidy; what else - oh yeah, I'll shove my desk chair out of the way: that's good enough," I postulate.

"It's totally sick; PIKES PEAK RUSH and MOON RAIDER conversion kits are currently available for this model while the ABYSSAL CHARGE and MARS DROP will be released soon. If this one's a gas, I'll try all of them," I gloat expectantly while grinning from ear to ear.

"Let's see what the user's manual says; *the simulator and all exo-accessories are wireless connected; when the orange button flashes, press it - the systems will synchronise and are enabled when the green light comes on. Please make sure the area adjacent to the simulator is clear of loose objects and packaging. Put the exoskeleton vest, gloves and flippers and the headpiece on (in the open position). Then step into the interactive flipper platforms and lean face forward against the upper-body floatation locator as illustrated. WHEN YOU'RE IN POSITION, CLOSE THE HEADPIECE. The simulator will automatically enter swimming mode.*"

There's a faint whirr as the system adjusts and I'm instantly immersed in an underwater scene.

"Wow, I'm an aqualung diver floating in a shallow sea with the hiss of my scuba gear and the rumble of expelled air bubbling to the surface. Hey-yaye, I'm swimming with flipper and glove actions too." Then a voice tells me, *'You're starting in level 1 in a quieter scenario away from the reef until you are familiar with the interactive controls and to establish a personal profile. Eye, head, body and limb movements interact with the game so you'll enjoy a realistic in-sea experience. Pressing the yellow cuff band on the left hand switches the SPOTLIGHT on to reveal the true colours of the reef and again for off; pressing the red band for CAMERA snaps or hold for 30 seconds of VIDEO that'll be printed at the end of the game. Pressing the black waistband will add or remove a virtual SPEARGUN in your hand with finger actions firing the spear and CLENCHING BOTH HANDS firmly will STOP THE GAME. GOOD LUCK; Press the orange cuff band on the right hand to START the action, please respect the reef and its inhabitants at all times.'* "No going back now good fellow; it's orange for go."

The seascape around me comes to life as a large Green Turtle brushes past as if I'm part of the scenery, a curious school of fingerlings mill around and a massive coral wall is visible through the green/blue hue.

"Juvenile Trevally I think," I guess from a good knowledge of reef fish. Then a surfer's wisdom dictates; practice some scuba manoeuvres so you'll be less awkward when the game gets tougher."

With that, I swim left and right, up and down, and for an emergency, some foot flipper torpedo escapes to gain confidence.

For a seasoned swimmer like me it comes naturally so I glance around to see what's happening, "Ha-hah, that's a dream scene; two Dugongs grazing on seagrass. It's a great opportunity for camera close-ups."

They're totally committed to munching seabed greens so I'm quickly into position and taking some fantastic shots. I'm watching a pair of master cultivators create sand clouds as they uproot the seagrass with magnificent autonomy.

"Who wouldn't be totally chuffed by that and I'm half expecting those sea cows to go moo-oo too. Anyhow, the reef is my next port of call; everything happens there. Uh-hol! What's sneaking up on me?"

Looking back, I'm eyeballing a big-big fish: it has white scales with grey/green spots.

"Hor-hor, you'd be a friendly Potato Cod, a solid citizen of the reef who's checking me out," I joke while attempting to stroke it.

It tolerates one touch, opens its mouth to display an array of teeth as if it's saying 'do you mind', then lazily swings out of reach and heads for the reef.

"Skews me, not keen on affection today, aye?"

I'm turning to follow that aquatic heavyweight when spoken instructions distract me, *'Beep, beep; you've graduated from level 1 and can enact games 2-7 and difficulty settings 1-3 for an enhanced format where points are added for avoiding hazards or deducted for injury. Press the purple patch on the back of your right hand to select the game 2-7 and the green patch for difficulty 1-3. Keep in mind most corals are armed with stinging cells or poisonous spikes as a defence or for catching prey.'*

"Whoopee, bring it on; the tougher the better. I'll try level 5, difficulty 2," my ego talks while initiating the settings.

'Beep, beep, please note; it's your goal to negotiate the reef without injury and earn 12000 points for a perfect game. Coral or creature stings are -100 points, body contact injury -500 points etc. Getting snagged, a life threatening injury or being swept away by a channel current, both feet off the flipper platforms together and/or dislodged exo-gear incurs -20000 points and is end of game. Level 7 is a night dive to witness the true miracle of coral spawning at a living reef. Each dive is one-hour maximum so consult your wrist dive watch and depth gauge regularly and swim to the surface when it's in the red sector or you won't finish the game. Wave a hand in front of your goggles for an aggregate points score and dive-time left.'

The scenario instantly changes, I find myself at the entrance to a reef lagoon, where the sun window above radiates a mosaic of changing light patterns on the white coral rubble. Sculptured coral walls that team with a myriad of brightly coloured fish flank me.

"Brother, its spectacular! I'd like to come back as a dolphin in another lifetime and enjoy this natural eye candy all the time. It's truly immense so touring the lagoon is an obvious choice."

Then my first challenge appears. I'm traversing the entrance channel when a small frumpy fish is suddenly in my face and determined to occupy the same patch of ocean.

"Come on little fella, move aside," I object while attempting to shepherd it aside.

It reacts by inflating into a spiky ball of bristles twice its original size.

"Okay, o-okay Puffer Fish; have it your way. I don't need to lose points on your behalf. Chee; there's all this sea and the little tacker wants to be difficult. I'll check out the coral high-rise instead."

The mammoth thickets of spiky armour, stacked shelfs and dark labyrinths amaze me. I've briefly glimpsed this world before; surfing wipe-outs have dumped me on the sea floor but it's never been as beautiful as this. "It could be the inshore palace of an ancient sea god; encrusted tiered castles, jeweled towers and embroidered temples amongst white/green porcelain forests and fluorescent impasto gardens with a royal guard swimming the daily drill in their ceremonial uniform. It's a vast subterranean dormitory with a hierarchy of colourful inhabitants living around it. Isn't it fantastic that all this grandeur is in one place?"

Then I spot a living arrangement that always intrigued me. Switching the spotlight on, I close in to examine the soft green tentacles of an Anemone.

"Hello, shy Clown Fishes, I can see how those stinging cells camouflage and protect you; a live-in cleaner in return for favours, aye. Mmm, something's moving inside that dark hole behind you. A-agh! A blessed Moray Eel wants a meal but it won't be me," I yell as its beady eyes and gaping jaws shoot out towards me.

"Yikes! You're bloody quick," I scream while defensively jerking my arm back. "Probably thinks my limb's a rival eel invading its coral fortress; I might spear a fish and bring it back as a peace offering. Let's see; what's hiding behind that soft coral sprawl further up the reef slope."

Ready for some sport I select the spear gun and slowly torpedo swim above the coral thickets. When my flipper clips a blue coral it responds instantly; a mass of purple/blue polyps withdraw into its convoluted skeleton. That reveals a brace of live-in shrimps and attracts a host of bigger fish.

"You-bewdy, a lucky fisher I might be," I'm thinking aloud and aiming at a Coral Cod that darts from an encrusted hollow to nab an easy meal. "Drat it, the spear just missed; maybe next time."

Then a shoal of decorous fish engulfs me, stoically holding station they're seemingly entranced by this air bubbling intruder. Below me, a squad of sentry smart Butterfly Fish play hide and seek behind finely crocheted gorgonian fans. While nearby, Angelfish zoom around bright red hydroid coral lattices like a well-rehearsed troupe in an ocean waltz. Then my wish is granted; I spot a young Tiger Trout. It's sheltering behind some clustered tubular sponges in a shallow gutter.

"Whoa-ho, I'm sure that eel would love a fresh treat," My adrenalin kicks in while aiming and firing the spear. "Howzat! A bullseye this time; I'll swim back and make amends with that feisty carnivore."

Unfortunately, a couple of sleek grey shapes scythe in from nowhere and abruptly interrupt the journey back with that bleeding fish on my spear. "Yowl! Damn ravenous White-Tipped Sharks; get the hell away from my catch," my anger spills forth while desperately jabbing the empty spear gun at them, then slipping the now tail-less fish between two coral clumps to protect it. "I'll torpedo swim to the bottom of the reef wall and deliver it pronto."

"Get outa my way; get outa here you danged things," I growl, while fending off those pesky sharks as they menace and shade me all the way to the eel's coral fortress. "Heck, just made it," I gasp through some heavy breathing while presenting my catch. "Please accept this appeasement for intruding in your reef territory so nature can smile on me again," I plead, as the moray eel cautiously snatches that tasty morsel from my gloved hand.

Then an imposing silhouette glides down from above and around me as if I'm part of the coral sculpture.

"Now that's a perfect answer, a Hawksbill Turtle has arrived to guide me around the reef. Maybe I can hitch a ride." I'm thinking while swimming after it.

"Gee, I can't hack its pace." A tad dejected I grumble, as that shielded creature disappears over a coral wall. "That danged thing sped up; keep your eyes open mate and you might get another chance."

"Let's see who's out of sight and out of mind; that encrusted plate tower should be a convenient squat for night feeders." My curiosity urges me to peer into the dark gaps. "Ah-ha, I spy antenna and lots of spiny legs; yum, I love lobster tail, it's so delish. Oh pity, it's just a particolored Mantis Shrimp with its stunning claws armed and ready for a fight. The little tacker will be gutsy and brave so I'll leave it be"

I'm about to move on when my hand brushes past a dark hollow. Two rainbow-banded fish suddenly appear and dart back and forth aggressively.

"Jeepers, you'd be Harlequin Tusk fish for sure; those prominent teeth are a dead give-away. You're certainly not frightened of me but I think that fierce look belies your beauty."

"Well I'll be, I'm graced by some happy looking company for a change, a school of Sweetlips are pouring over the reef and their smiling demeanour pleases me too. Oh my, they've swarmed between a group of tiny Puller's and the reef so its instant takeaway; ouch, all gone."

A surfer's intuition or possibly a hint of movement in the corner of my eye makes me reflex around to face danger.

"Yow! A Box Jellyfish, the most lethal stinger of the tropics. If I'd blundered into that hooded ghost and copped a tentacle wrap, it would've been a painful end for sure. All the same, one must admire the pure simplicity of a phantom medusa that has no brain or heart to guide its endeavours. It can have this friggin patch of sea to itself; I'll checkout that staghorn cluster next door."

Treading water for a while, I admire the mammoth thickets of entangled coral tusks and antlers that salute the sun's rays and watch a Hermit Crab as it traverses an adjacent coral plate. All of a sudden, something pounces from a hollow but retreats just as fast.

"What in the heck is happening there," I wonder while swimming low over the spot. "Oh my, a clever little crustacean is hosting a small anemone on its shell as an active defence."

I'm intrigued, that ambush attacker got more than it bargained for; it's worth a squiz to see who it is.

"Well I'll be danged, some real time Octopus action in the wild; it's time for a little photo fun I reckon, he-he." I chuckle; selecting the camera and spotlight while dropping into position outside its hidey-hole. Jeepers, that camouflage is spot on, it could be a rock if I didn't know better. Please move along little fella, don't lie doggo on me." I nudge it and take a nice shot. "By-jingo, it's blushing in waves of red to purple, a tad upset and angry at being found aye? Come on; (prodding with my finger while video mode is switched on) I'd love to record a reef Houdini squeezing in and out of coral crevices. Mm-m, not in the mood pal; I'll take a close up instead." Then there's a sudden surprise as I zoom in. "A-agh, it's making a jet escape; oh dear, its inky black cloud enshrouds me so I can't see where it's gone."

Unfortunately, my left flipper digs in and creates a sandy fog while the other clobbers a bottom dwelling Sea Cucumber.

"U-ur! Its disgorged gut organs have slimed my flippers and the adjacent coral. Sorry Mr Cewy, I didn't mean it. You have a right to defend yourself." I try to atone by righting it. "Hah-hah! Oh boy, that's the funniest over-reaction I've ever seem!" A weird moment to savour I think while flicking the mess off.

Then I suddenly realise that all the large fish have vanished so I look around. *"BLOODY HELL, A TIGER SHARK!"* A shock wave of fear makes me duck behind a massive brain coral; the only hint of cover nearby. Its cool countenance intimidates a usually confident me as it cruises past a mere arm span or two away.

"Thank goodness it's not in a preying mood but ignoring that icy glare could be perilous," I consider carefully, as its lithe streamlined form glides up over the reef and disappears from view.

The reef activity returns and as my nerves settle, I scan the upper reef for a new feature to explore and there's a large crevasse I can swim into. The entrance is lined with swaying mauve, blue and green soft corals amongst a low forest of brilliant red, orange and yellow hard coral fans; their polyp blooms are open and filtering plankton from the current.

"That colourful display is worth a closer look and there's a cave to explore as well." I think while heading straight for it. My only obstacle is a shoal of bright blue Damsel Fish hovering in and around the spiky branches of an adjacent coral mound. Suddenly one of them charges at my arm.

"Struth, the little mite's harassing me," I cry while backpedalling and inadvertently treading on a Stingray half-buried in the coral sand. "Heck! Its tail-barb nearly stabbed me as it flapped around and scooted away."

My sudden awkwardness startles a group of Bearded Trigger Fish who dart for sanctuary in a massive stalky staghorn. That prompts me to look back and there's a very slippery critter approaching from behind.

"Yikes; an Olive Sea Snake is hot on my tail," a wave of panic hits me. "They're venomous; I'd better make myself scarce inside that crevasse."

Unfortunately, that sea serpent catches up so I stop and face it.

"Lummy, I know your kind's attracted to human divers. Hey! That's close enough, you might bite me." Distraught, I try to shepherd it away. "Oh-No! Don't coil around my leg you persistent devil; plea-ease unwind and go cuddle a fish, crab or anything else you fancy. Aa-agh, I'm defenceless and sinking to the seafloor; phew, it's losing interest and slipping off, thank goodness for that, by-ye."

In an effort to catch my breath and steady a few frazzled nerves I tread water once more and watch the serpent's reef hunting tactics. The reptile checks out several hollows or hideaways before it scores a shrimp and swallows it, ascends to refill its lungs, then dives again and disappears into a connecting reef alley. "Others might call that a fishy love-hug but it surely put the wind up me."

In an effort to avoid trouble for a bit, I decide to reconnoitre that crevasse."

"Isn't that cute, a big school of Yellow-Banded Hussar's, smaller numbers of orange Fairy Basslets and some Green Pullers are hovering on the current and are completely unfazed by me. Uh-hol, they're giving a wide berth to a Coral Trout that's approaching us. I'd say that wily predator is mocking them with a spontaneous yawn of its toothy jaws because it's not hungry."

Not wanting to interfere I give it room by gently stroking and flippering backwards onto an encrusted rock. I'm utterly shocked when it comes alive, rears up and snaps at me.

"Yah-hah! I nearly stomped on a Wobbegong Shark; it could have held on till I drowned; yours truly can't take a trick at the moment. That's unusual, twinkling lights in the deep recesses;

there aren't any stars or min-mins down here. I'll have to investigate."

Swimming deeper I encounter a dark hollow jam-packed with snoozing Cardinal Fish; they're so quaint I decide to leave them be. Switching the spotlight on I go further into that narrowing space until I find my quarry.

"How do you like that, spooky little blackfishes with a glowing organ and shutter brow below their eyes for switching light signals on and off? They'd be Flashlight Fish, night-time feeders that are rarely seen. That's enough coral caving, I wonder what's going on outside?"

Escaping the darkness, I swim to the top of the sunlit reef to survey the action in both the lagoon and adjacent channels.

"Haa-haaa, that speedster turtle is munching on seagrass further down the channel but the bugger's likely to zip away if I go chasing it. "Watch out fast flippers, there's an oceanic-tiger on the prowl and you're its favourite food."

Then I notice big clusters of yellow, orange or red Feather Stars on the coral outcrop below. I'm aware of their nifty secret; they look like plants but they're actually animals. They climb or float to plankton hotspots so their fern like arms can intercept those current-borne snacks.

"By jingo, that's a surreal scene; a black rolling wave is creating a sand cloud in the lagoon. I'll be darned; it's thousands of tightly knit Catfish in a head-down dance. They're all racing to front of the queue for an instant feast; nature's seafloor cleaner is a bewdy, aye. Oh boy, it's a magical day when a red'n'white Spanish Dancer, the only swimming mollusc with a flamenco style flapping skirt is heading towards me; I'll be patient and see where it goes. Ah-ha, it's landed on a tubular sponge; its preferred food I'd say." Then, intuition makes me turn around and to my delight, a small pod of natural surfing companions are entering the lagoon.

"That's clever. The Dolphins are herding a shoal of Trevally fingerlings towards the channel wall and one at a time they're scything through that writhing mass for a feed; an oceanic takeaway I'd say."

Then two of that playful group break free and chase a large Red Emperor for some carefree sport; Panic-stricken, it dodges and weaves all over that open space until it finds sanctuary in a coral bommie. Undeterred the dolphins continue their frivolous odyssey, skimming across the lagoon's undulating floor, then up through a coral arch, along the reef's crest and back into the lagoon again. While this is happening, I've sunk to the sandy bottom for an impromptu photo shoot of their life games.

"Gee, they're having a ball; it'd be marvellous to swim like those oceanic danseurs. Those sleek beauties are heading in my direction; Hor-hor, its action flick time," I celebrate while crouching low and selecting video mode.

"That's it my movie stars, give me your natural smiling pose and perform some aquatic tricks for my audience please."

As if following an unwritten script the duo continues their light-hearted tour of the lagoon with upside down swims, loop the loops and barrel rolls in unison before heading back to me.

"Perfect, a front-on shot would be wonderful," I secretly wish as they glide down straight for me while emitting their clicking lingo so I need to back up a step or two. "You're certainly not human shy," I say while stroking the closest. Then, as if satisfied that I'm friendly, they swim away, turn back, then swim away slowly. "Are you saying this is the life; come join in the fun? Well, I might just do that."

Launching into a slow freestyle I follow suit and to my surprise, they double back to be my swimming buddies. Totally spent after we've half skirted the lagoon, I drop behind and watch their seamless hijinks of body-rolls, pirouettes or dives with just a little envy.

"Ok-ok, you're the master, I'm the apprentice and it's your playground; go and join your oceanic mates," I say goodbye as the pod ascend and quickly disappear into the crystal blue waves rolling over the reef. Taking their lead, I torpedo swim up and above the reef to admire the coral polyp's mastery and the awesome scope of their work. Then right on cue, some familiar silhouettes cruise in near the surface so I'm expecting a flurry of activity.

"No guessing them, Barracuda's; our speedsters of the reef waters. It'd be nice to see their feeding style but don't mess with 'em mate," I remind myself of a past incident. "Yeah, I was trying to extract a hook from one of your cousin's gills when it wriggled violently and its danged razor teeth lacerated my little finger."

Their silver/grey scales glint in the sunlit surface sea and they seem unperturbed by my presence. Then a large one suddenly darts towards the reef.

"Wow, that Spotted Hawkfish got nailed, it didn't have time to react."

Quite frankly, I'm feeling rather vulnerable in the clear water above the reef. That prompts me to dive but suddenly, I'm front-on to the whopp'n great mouth of a Whale Shark.

"Ah-ho! A maxi slo-mo filter feeder; it certainly won't bite me to death but it could run me down softly, I reckon. You're a gentle sub-mariner that loves gliding through our plankton rich reef waters, aye. I'll tag along like your entourage of hanger's-on, if you don't mind big bro."

I enjoy its magnificence as far as the reef drop-off and gesture au revoir as it swings towards the deep, deep blue. Then I descend to the upper reaches of the reef and chancing upon a white cloud hanging over the coral, I have to check it out.

"It's a sure sign of dedicated reef cleaners and their daily grind for food and lodging. There's more maroon algae than a pro-active mob of Parrot Fish can handle I think."

I watch that diligent activity with great interest until an enormous shoal of Trevally engulfs my vantage point and that encourages me to move on. No doubt, they're enroute from the lagoon to the outer slope for an afternoon's feeding.

Then a fin-tastic silvery/bronze ocean sunfish draws my attention as it sails past, homes in on a coral outcrop and hesitates there. "Obviously the local cleansing station," I guess, after observing several black striped fish dart out, then pop in and around its mouth, gills or fins whilst their host is motionless. Their last customer, a large Humphead Wrasse has left the grooming area and is gliding along the reef when it suddenly attacks a Crown of Thorns Starfish.

"Oh no, dead coral; that fish knows the culprits," my anger builds as I look further afield; immediately spotting the likely suspects on a nearby table coral. "Blasted things; the spear gun's get'n a workout now."

Silly me, I'm taking aim at point blank range when a careless flipper stroke sees my leg brush against that offending starfish. "Ouch, you might have sharp defences against me and other foe but not against this macho weapon," I bark while pulling the trigger. "Ha-a; exit one coral destroyer." Then I swiftly pass judgement on another two nearby to finish the job. "Sayonara devil starfish" and "Bon voyage to hell", I declare victory.

However, when I scan the coral scenery the reality sinks in; that enemy is everywhere but a glimmer of hope is in view.

"Well I'll be; nature's fighting back too. A spiral triton shell is devouring one of those obnoxious pests; it's just a solitary ally but a welcome sight anyway."

Extracting some revenge has lifted my spirit quite a bit so I power-stroke down an adjacent coral hall to clear my thoughts. A large school of Paddle-Tail Hussars are up ahead and because there's no easy way past I'm forced to burst through their ranks. Before me is an awesome sight.

"Wow, a graceful Manta Ray filter-feeding train; a flotilla of undersea flyers doing circuits of the channel, flapping, gliding and turning about in one graceful move. Swimming with those friendly giants is a scuba diving dream."

"Let's see, it'll be much easier to join in where they turn about - well I'll be, isn't that a happy coincidence; my friend the speedy Turtle is heading this way. A Turtle ride beside the Manta Rays would be a double Geronimo, aye."

Its target is a seagrass clump down below and a table coral is just above it so I quickly swim into a hidden position; now I'm poised to spring an ambush.

"Ah-huh: GOTCHA! Hor-hor, this aquatic beast's flipper power is so strong; shifting my body weight is the only way to steer it. I'll go down as the first undersea buckaroo to train a shell-back thoroughbred. We'll follow that Manta train, if you please HT. Soon we're in sync with those stealthy wings of the sea and it seems like a magical ride in scuba heaven to be alongside those gliding Manta's as they filter-feed on the plankton sea-soup. However, my joy is short-lived when they turnabout for another run and no matter how I try, my flippered steed won't follow suit. Luckily, I'm rewarded by a glimpse of something truly special so I dismount and swim for the reef once more.

"Thank you bro-Turtle, a super fabulous tow it was; BON VOYAGE!" I wish it well. "Struth, the tide must be going out; fight this persistent current mate or become ocean bait," is my almost panicking thought while desperately stroking towards the nearest shelter, a huge mushroom coral on the reef wall.

Once I'm behind that living monolith the next challenge must be considered; getting to the other side of this seaward surge. I watch a school of Red Snapper zip past really fast as if it's their tidal expressway.

"Phew, I'll have to be cautious from now on," my thoughts decree while peering down that sandy-floored alley at a rustic shape melded into the coral.

"Wowee; a dream find for any scuba freak, a once proud schooner entombed by the sea. The keel must be 30 metres long and the bow is firmly wedged between two massive staghorn stands so its name is nature's secret for now. At least its encrusted backbone, dinosaur ribs and stern are exposed to the briny for my exploration."

It seems good fortune is smiling on me; the shattered wreck almost blocks the alley's entrance. After building up some bravado, I entered that untamed current and rode the surging outflow until the encrusted remains are within reach, then grabbing hold of an exposed rib, I hauled myself aboard. Now safely inside the hull it's obvious that both decks have collapsed onto the keel and little else is intact.

What a pity it's in such a mess, a least the ships wooden wheel and metal base are intact and resting against the amidships ribs, all suitably encased in algae and barnacles. It might be a piece of nautical treasure if it turns," I reason before giving it a heave-to. "Huh-agh! Nah, its frozen solid, the mountings are well and truly anchored in the coral as well."

Then, letting go and leaning back to drift away, my helmet hits something that wasn't there a moment ago; it was an empty hull. Startled, packing it and twisting around, I'm staring into the eyeballs of a huge stony-faced Grouper that seems to be asking, "What're you disturbing in my territory buddy?"

"Yow! Hi reef-chief, n-need some c-company," I stammer while retreating a bit.

Realising it's a great photo opportunity; I switch the spotlight and video on to record the drama of this encounter for posterity as that huge fish studies me. Then, curiosity satisfied or losing interest, it slowly turns and slips almost lazily from the confines of the wreck.

"Adieu great friend," I salute its non-aggressive courtesy before continuing my exploration of the hull.

It seems as if I've found a secret garden with an exotic centre piece, a Giant Clam; its bright green and purple mantle looks like an enormous flower that is ready to blossom. Surrounding it are red, yellow or orange clusters of chimney sponges, pink/purple open vases or pockmarked fans; a random display that covers all the deck debris and exposed ribs.

"It's beautiful in its own way, the oceanic equivalent of the cactus and succulent garden at home," I ponder while watching a small piece of sponge literally walk towards a tiny fish. "I'd say that's an Anglerfish with a dangling lure ready to... ouch, it's got a meal."

Then a large sail like Batfish enters the confines of the hull and hovers above every coral and sponge as it moves along the keel. It could be looking for a place to lay its eggs so I move in for a close-up picture but I spook it instead - as a result, the fish disappears behind a broken bulkhead. Upon looking, it has escaped through a gaping hole torn in the bow.

"That'll teach me to be more patient if I want the best shots. Then I'm aware of a sharp snapping sound; where is it coming from, who the devil is making it?" that unfamiliar background echo puzzles me so I listen for its source.

Without warning, there's a burst of activity on the reef wall beside the bow and that conspicuous echo is there again so I calmly watch the situation. Suddenly, a Yellow-Striped Fusilier strays from the coral and is charged down by a Silver Trevally, then snap, snap - it's noisily scored for a meal.

"Another problem solved, it's time to move on," crosses my mind as I peruse the channel's mood before heading back. The outflow seems to have abated somewhat so it must be the top of the tide and that suits me. I'm about to re-enter that tamed current when there's an explosion of movement nearby; instantly involving me as an unwilling player in a horror drama.

"Hells Bells! I'll be wild fish food," I'm suddenly in panic mode and bracing to defend. Three White-Tipped Sharks have driven half a dozen Tuna into the reef channel and cornered them against the wreck. With ruthless looping charges, they commence a feeding frenzy that puts me into high-risk territory. "Keep away you savage beasts," I scream while flipper lunging defensively as one streaks towards me; fortunately it passes beneath my legs without attacking.

"Retreat or be a red meat feast," my inner-alarm commands me to swim behind the hull's encrusted ribs for the scant shelter they provide. "Phew, do I have to watch my back or what?"

Then one of the Tuna charges inside the hull but gets nailed in a top corner, forcing me to fend off and dodge the shark's thrashing tail. "Aa-aagh! Who'd want to be a sporting fish?" I anxiously think as a tailless head and torn flesh float down beside me. Fortunately, the calmness returns when the two surviving tuna escape and head for the open sea with the sharks in hot pursuit.

"Boy-o-boy, I can't tarry here any longer," this uneasy aquanaut worries while checking the reef scene once more. Then, consulting my dive watch I slip into sensory overload, "Damn thing, it's in the red sector danger zone, I'll have to resurface like pronto."

"It's now or never," my anxiety takes over while slipping into the channel and after a flurry of urgent strokes; I hesitate to locate the base ship's shadow on the sunlit surface. Then my sixth sense makes me look back. *GORBLIMEY! THAT TIGER SHARK HAS RETURNED AND IT'S BETWEEN ME AND MY LAST HIDING SPOT.*" I'm suddenly in shock; I need to go up and into the open. What can I do?

"*Oh Dear, excited vibes from that last feeding frenzy have attracted it,*" I realise and head for the only hint of shelter nearby; a large pair of gorgonian coral fans. Their open-weave lattice is no protection to speak of but it's an obstacle between me and my aggressive foe.

"*Is this my bitter end,*" I ponder; a victim's terror hits home as it cruises past with jerky body moves, a cold steely glare and lethal toothy grin. Then, sharply swinging in an arc it comes back head-on, displaying every bit of jaw armoury and giving me a hungry look as it skims over that flimsy coral barricade.

"Pull yourself together matey, when you're dumped by a monster wave it has sharp teeth too," my fighting spirit kicks in. Then as the adrenalin of fear sets in a bright idea hits me, *"I'll counter-attack with my own weaponry."* In a flash I've switched the spear gun on and kicked around to face the enemy but my flipper slips off the coral plate. *"OOOOOW!"* I feel an excruciating stab of pain as its jagged edge tears into my shin. *"That stinging gash must be bleeding bad; OH GEEZ! Where has that crafty devil gone; over the reef so it can unleash a sneak attack?"* my horrified mind thinks until a glimmer of hope reappears; it might not return or maybe it'll score a large fish and leave via the lagoon. Then, after glancing at my dive watch another chill of panic invades me; stay here and drown or resurface fast and be at the mercy of this marauding enemy.

"OH DEAR, BIG TROUBLE'S AT HAND." I complain aloud while staring nervously as scores of fish pour out from between two staghorn coral mounds and scatter in every direction. My greatest dread suddenly appears and heads my way. It ignored me earlier on but it's probably in a feasting mood this time. *"DAMN! It's zooming in from the side with a wisp of my blood slick guiding it in."*

"I ACCEPT YOUR CHALLENGE TIGE; IT'S ONE ON ONE NOW!" I shout a warning while aiming the spear gun as those beastly gaping jaws thrust towards me like a homing torpedo.

With my trigger finger ready, I wait, *'HOLD-HOLD-HOLD-FIRE!'* before diving across the soft coral on the reef slope behind me; then all hell breaks loose. The coral I'm landing on collapses… then *'OO-OW-AAGH'*, my side is racked with excruciating pain." (Suddenly everything goes black)

"That's funny; I should've been a shark's dinner this time. (frantically feeling everywhere for injuries) I seem to be in one piece but my side aches from that almighty thump and my leg is stinging like crazy; I must be alive and not in the after-life! I WON, HOORAY! HAA-HAA, I WON!"

Then a message flashes before me -

A MAJOR REEF INCIDENT ENDED YOUR GAME.

Your total score was 6200 pts of a possible 12000 pts. The design crew at Virtl Xplorr are delighted that you embraced their challenge and hope the experience was enjoyable.

PLEASE OPEN YOUR HEADPIECE TO SETUP FOR THE NEXT GAME. ADDITIONALLY: *IF YOU WISH TO CONTINUE PLAYING, EACH NEW GAME FEATURES A DIFFERENT REEF AND DIVE SENARIO FOR ADDED EXCITEMENT.*

"Click"

"Bret, we're back from Aspen. Are you here Bret?"

"I think so…"

"Bret, are you OK, what happened…? Hold on. I'll get dad."

"Ron, is that you?"

"Dad, Bret's fallen off the simulator and is on the floor, he might be hurt…"

"What do you mean, he's injured? Is he still conscious son? Get your mum from the car please. **BRET - speak to me fella; are you alright?"**

"I-I might be but it's all black."

"Thank goodness, you're still coherent. I'll open the headpiece so you can see us matey. Don't move for a minute - we need to know if you're okay."

"Steve! Phew, that shark had my number until I shot it at point-blank range with my spear gun and launched onto some soft coral - reckon I won that fight, aye!"

"It looks like your computer system was in the wars too, matey; but that doesn't matter, are you alright? Your leg's bleeding badly; how's the rest of you? Joan's here now, she'll check you out."

"Yeah, the corner of that open drawer has blood dripping off of it dad."

"Oh dear, what made this happen Bret. Your shin needs some urgent attention; are there any other aches and pains, son."

"My side is pretty sore - just here."

"Pull his exo-vest out of the way Steve; mm-m looks like a decent bruise is forming but I can't feel anything broken Bret. Okay boys, help me to lift and sit Bret on that chair and remove all the exo-gear; then we'll take it from there. How are you feeling love?"

"Aside from a wounded pride I'm pretty right. The action is super sick - There I was, in a life and death struggle with a tiger shark when everything went black."

"Bret, it seems the game ended when you jumped from the simulator. Then you grabbed the monitor as you fell and that pulled the computer tower down on top of you too. A little damage aside we'll get you fixed up first; a med-check is next. I'll send your macho machine back to Explorr Studios son."

"Fair go Steve; real surfers conquer the ocean's most daring waves; it's the same for scuba dives. It's the real deal - an extreme excitement machine that's great for honing my underwater skills. I'll use it again and again, and I can't wait to play the other games as well."

"Yeah me too; I'm just as keen as my big bro, dad."

"OK-OK, it can stay but it's straight to the clinic for now Bret."

For the majority of our human existence the depths of the ocean have been an unknown factor because exploration was beyond the equipment of the day. However, modern research has revealed the intriguing behaviour of whales, giant squids and deep-water fishes in that dark secretive environment. This new knowledge is the genesis for a dramatic and emotional story about the ambivalence between one of those elusive creatures and a crusty mariner.

Conversely, there is a wealth of knowledge available about the unique creatures that live in and around our coral reefs. However, scuba divers need only apply for a firsthand visit so that led to a story about a young student's sojourn into virtual reality. Using a futuristic simulator, he's a scuba diver in a reef game that challenges his ability to survive, especially when there's a twist of fortunes.

www.ingramcontent.com/pod-product-compliance
Lightning Source LLC
Chambersburg PA
CBHW070810120626
46557CB00002B/802